SQUARES IN MY CIRCLE

A PRETTY SAVAGE LUST STORY

KEISH MONIQUE

STAY LOW STACK PAPER PUBLISHING

ISBN: 979-8-9876053-0-1 (Print)

ISBN: 979-8-9876053-1-8 (eBook)

1st Edition

Published by Stay Low Stack Paper Publishing

Los Angeles, CA

staylowstackpaper.com

I dedicate this to all my Boss Ladies making a way out of no way. It's not easy, but we make it look good!

CONTENTS

CHAPTER 1
ANGLES

"Why do I even deal with this fool
and her always smiling ass, a
mess…"

"COME FOR ME BABY", Bleu moaned as her tongue deep-dived in my ocean, while looking up at me dead in my eyes. She always had a funny way of telling me she loved me. And an even better way of showing it.

But it felt so good that I had to look away to hold that nut a little bit longer. Shit, it felt so good that I had to get it on video.

So, I reached over to get my red Super Alpha 14, the one with all the fucking cameras from off her paisley navy-blue comforter.

Then I swiped left to open up the camera app before hitting all those angles, just right. I just had to get this on camera for future reference for when she isn't here to satisfy my needs.

Bleu saw and smiled with her freaky ass, before staring into the camera lens, softly saying, *"I thought I told you come for me, baby."*

It was at that point I felt my legs start to do that involuntary movement thing and my hands pushing Bleu's head further down the… Then fuck, here goes that nigga Curtis calling, again.

Well, not that nigga. More like my boyfriend of the past two years. Curtis was his name and lame was his game. So, it didn't take twice for me to think to hit decline.

But I should've just let that shit ring and go straight to voicemail, because just as I was about to silence the call, Bleu's shady ass slid two fingers deep inside, causing me to accidentally accept Curtis' video call. Right around the same time I was coming. Hard.

I was screaming, Curtis was yelling *"What the fuck, yo!"*, and Bleu was smiling like "yeah nigga, I got yo girl".

Why do I even deal with this fool and her always smiling ass, a mess. Why am I still with that lame ass nigga too? The only reason I stick around is because he's the most stable person in my life right now.

Shit, how am I going to explain all of this when I get home. But I had to think about all that later because Bleu's wife just sent a text that she got off early and was on her way home to get broke off.

"How could we not be fire when fuckin'…"

CLICK CLACK. Click clack. Click clack… went my the bottom of my red heels, as I was making my way to the parking structure of Bleu's place. Hair all fucked up, one arm in my trench coat with the other holding on to my purse, hoping I didn't leave my keys upstairs.

"This shady ass bitch", I mumbled to myself, just thinking about how everything went down. How could she do me like that? I know she doesn't like Curtis and the way he talks to me sometimes. But damn, you don't do your Day 1 like that.

Besides the point, what's her wife doing getting off work early today anyway. I should be the one getting broke off. Not Wanda and her square ass. Her and Curtis should get together. I bet they'd have a good ol' time.

So, here I am now, weak in the knees from that good-ass nut, still looking for my keys. Fuck. I must've left them on the nightstand.

I'm just going to have to text Bleu and tell her to take the trash out or some shit, so she can slide me those keys. Because although I'm not looking forward to going home and hearing Curtis' mouth, it sure does beat sitting here reminiscing in my car for an hour straight.

"My keys are on the nightstand. Bring them out to me, now", is what the text message read. Wanda must not be there yet I thought, with the way those three dots went off right away.

"Hey bae, you mad at me?", Bleu typed with a sad face emoji. Although I knew damn well she was grinning on the other end of the phone.

But all I did was type "Run me my keys nigga!", so fast and hard I damn near broke a nail.

"Alright, alright. Wya?", Bleu responded 7 minutes later. Damn, Wanda must've got there early. So, I told Bleu to grab her trash and meet me in her penthouse's parking structure, ASAP.

So, here I am waiting by the entrance, fake scrolling through my phone, hoping nobody recognizes me looking like a damn fool.

12 more minutes pass and I finally see Bleu's fine ass

strolling with the quickness, which let me know she's got to head back upstairs before Wanda gets suspicious again.

So, I get my keys and a light tap on the butt with her diamond and gold-draped right hand before Bleu made her exit.

"*Call me later, bae*", she said so softly, so sexily… Omg, why do I love this woman! There's just something about her swag that I've always loved. Even when we had nothing…

Thank God I have my keys now though. Although I got those back, Bleu holds another set of keys that no one knows exists. Another set of keys that unlocks my deepest, inner freak.

Nobody can get me off like Bleu. We've known each other so long and explored each other's body and mind so thoroughly, how could we not be fire when fuckin'.

I said I wasn't going to sit here and reminisce though. So, I tossed my purse, trench coat, and phone into the passenger side of my matte black whip before starting her up.

But, before I reverse out of guest parking, let me give Alex a call to see what's up for the weekend.

"Who doesn't love someone that
hits you right back…"

(323) 867-5446… That's Alex's number or "Ace" in my contacts. You see, when Bleu isn't breaking me off or Curtis getting on my last got damn nerve, Ace is next in line for a lil' face time.

Although she can come across as a little shy when you first meet her, I'm glad I didn't let that shit fool me. Because lemme tell you… Alex knows how to make it do what it do.

"Hey bae, what's up for the weekend?", Alex answered on the second ring. That's what I love about her - she's not out here playing games like these ignant ass niggas, i.e., Bleu.

Who doesn't love someone that hits you right back and isn't into ego or mind games? Some people call it simpin', but I love that shit. Make a bitch feel wanted sometimes, ya know?

"Well, I was thinking we can head over to that place that just opened off Robertson and then Jax, before heading back to your place to do what we do. How does that sound?", I said in my most nonchalant voice.

"You know I'm always down to ride with you baby", Alex replied oh so eagerly. *"I'll be ready at 3. Want me to wear that lil' thing you like ..."*

Damn, damn, damn! Here goes that nigga Curtis calling, probably wondering why I haven't gave a damn to call or explain myself.

But he's right, I don't give a damn. If I had any more fucks to give they flowed out my pussy and right into Bleu's mouth a long time ago.

"Wait, hold on boo that's my other line."

"Damn nigga, what do you want?!", I yelled into the phone so loud an old lady passing in front of my truck shot me a dirty look. But who cares. She should know I don't give a fuck too.

"First off, don't come at me like that. I will come find yo ass and you won't like it. And second, why are you still fuckin' that nigga Bleu. You said you been deaded that shit."

Wow, I never heard Curtis sound this mad. Maybe I should call Alex back another time.

"Getting pussy is easy and dick
even less of a challenge when
you're that bitch…"

"DAMN, I gotta take this call. I'll hit you up a lil' later though", I said trying not to sound completely and utterly pissed off.

"It's ok bae, I know you're busy. Just call me back when you get a chance. Byeeee."

Wow. Maybe I should make Ace the one and not the two like her name implies. Because with the way this whole Curtis and Bleu situation is going, I might not have anyone to drown in my ocean.

Well, let me not take it that far, because I am the prize, the one and not the two. Getting pussy is easy and dick is even less of a challenge when you're that bitch

I wish more bitches would get that instead of chasing after these no-good ass niggas just because they have money, status, and maybe some good dick. And that's a hard with the maybe.

Sometimes I wonder what life would be like if I had a dick. Well, that's not much of a mystery though with the way I whip out that strap on Alex.

Click.

"Yes, Curtis. How may I help you?", I said with my eyes rolling so far back in my head they hurt a bit from the strain.

"BITCH, don't you ever disrespect me out here in these streets. You already know my sister and cousins will be up there on that ass before I can disconnect the call!"

OK. OK. "Disconnect the call". See, Curtis can be a lil' square at times. But I don't doubt him calling his goons for backup.

If this were my younger self, I would've proceeded to tell him where, when, why, and how he got me fucked up. But I digress.

"Nigga, I don't give a FUCK who you call up over here. They can all get it! You already know I don't play. But anyway, I'm sorry you had to see that. You know how you've been out of town a lot lately...

I just wasn't thinking straight, and those video sessions

weren't doing it for me anymore. I'd rather be safe than sorry. So, I went over to Bleu's… How can I make it up to you?"

Pause. Long pause, with an exasperated sigh at the end.

"Well, for starters you can delete that nigga's number out your phone. Then you can bring that ass home, open wide, and get these back shots."

Chills up and down my pussy.

"OK daddy. I'll be home soon."

"What good does that get you,
besides everything you already
got…"

BITCH, I'm 'bout to get some dick! I couldn't have pressed the brake pedal on Black Beauty to give her a start fast enough.

Good thing DTLA isn't that far from Studio City. Well, 20 minutes on a good day. But that's nothing compared to my daily commute from South Central to Santa Monica when I was working corporate.

God, I hated that job and am so glad I made the jump to be a boss years ago. How else could I afford to wine and dine the baddest baddies. They're expensive as fuck. At least the ones I like…

"Girl, turn around and bust it open. Let me go down and drown in your ocean", Buff serenaded as I queued up my sex playlist to get me in the mood.

All I know is it's about to go down soon as I get inside, like that Trust Johnson song. With the way Curtis has been in and out of town all year running his consulting business, it's like we're not even together. But when we're together it's nothing but busting back-to-back orgasms, with his ol' square ass.

I might talk a lot of shit about Curtis, but he's an alright guy. Probably one of the best to treat me in a while, which is why I'ma let him blow my back out tonight. All night.

I don't know about the whole deleting Bleu's number out my phone though. I'm not about to give up that mouth that easily. And I bet she's not trying to let me go that easily either.

"We can start on first base, 'til I knock that pussy out the park…"

Damn. Six tracks into "BangHers", and I'm already waiting for the door of our 3-car garage to open, so I can slide Black Beauty in.

I daydream entirely too much. Sometimes I wish I'd stay out my head and hop into reality more often. But what good does that get you, besides everything you already got.

Shit, I'm tired as fuck. That first nut with Bleu really

took me out. I don't know how I'm gonna washing machine trick, bust and twerk all on Curtis tonight.

I need a Purple Ostrich, Amp'd 4 Energy shot, or something!

"That was just my pussy talking
without consulting me first…"

I THOUGHT I was ready when I got off the phone, but that was just my pussy talking without consulting me first. Because if she did, I wouldn't be at this espresso machine right now hoping Curtis didn't hear me come in. And just to make sure he didn't, I made sure I took my heels off in the foyer.

Shit. Damn. Muthafucka. This coffee isn't doing a damn thing for me! Maybe I can just lay out on the sectional and act like work was too much again. Yeah, let me try that.

"I know you're not hiding from me, bae. Daddy's good girl has been very bad today. Come get your punishment."

Uh oh. Here comes Curtis down the stairs, in nothing but a towel. He must really be thinking I'm 'bout to go to work.

And I just might with the way his chocolate skin, v-cut abs, and perfectly groomed beard is poppin' tonight. Plus, he has his contacts in… girl.

It's really been too long since we got a good session in. It feels good to know he's not out here trickin' like these other lame-ass niggas. I know he better not.

"Get your ass over here", Curtis yelled out to me in front of our 85" TV, which I suddenly notice is set up to the camera and tripod.

See, what nobody knows is me and Curtis do PeekingFans on the side. Just for fun, you know. Because we definitely don't need the money.

"Yes Daddy", I moaned, taking off one piece of clothing with each step closer. First my mocha CCM belt. Then my AyeBaevon blouse… bra… panties. Until there was nothing left, on either one of us.

By the time I got on my knees to please, Curtis was so hard I thought he would bust before I got to do what I do. But he held that nut in good before pulling out and turning me around like he needed it, which I know he did.

Smacking my ass, then rubbing it down. Feeling me firmly from the front before slowing sliding in the back. Letting the slow stroke build up into a deep pound until we both busted so hard, we blacked out.

Phone ping. Oops... I forgot all about my boo Alex. I'll call her in the morning.

CHAPTER 7
EXPENSIVE APOLOGIES

"I hope my team doesn't notice me
walking in a lil' funny…"

FUCKKKK. Why is it already Monday, again? I'm no doubt thankful for another day. But Mondays are always the worse. Especially if I was getting my back blown out over the weekend.

Thank God I'm my own boss these days. Thank God for social media too. Without it, I'd still be at that fuck ass job pushing papers and fake smiling my way to the water cooler. Did I mention that I hated that job?

The six figures, company car, and all-expense paid trips were nice though. Can't front about that. It's funny how these jobs pay you just enough to feel comfortable and not leave, but not enough to feel satisfied.

Speaking of satisfaction, let me hit my boo back and see what's up for the weekend.

Ring. Ring. Ring. Ring, again. Voicemail.

"Hey bae, sorry we couldn't link up. Something came up and I was down all weekend. I want to make it up to you. Let me know how."

Damn. I hope Alex isn't too mad about it. But, after what Curtis did to me... I'm surprised I got out the bed this morning.

I hope my team doesn't notice me walking in a lil' funny. But then again, oh well. We're all grown up in this bitch and the checks still get signed the same.

Ring. Ring. *"Hey boo. You got my voicemail?"*

"Yeah, good morning. I got it", Alex replied so dry and coldly I thought I was on the phone with my ex, Mecca.

"You could've at least let me know you weren't going to make it. I was looking forward to seeing and being with you. I feel like you're always flaking on me, and it's not right", Alex went on.

Damn. I hate when she gets like this. Damn. I hate that me, her, and Curtis can't get together to explore the poly possibilities.

Maybe I should tell her about how me and him got engaged last winter. But it's too soon to spring it on her like that. I know Alex loves me and I'm starting to see I have deep feelings for her too.

I might be a pretty savage, but when you love someone, you don't do them dirty. Or whatever Londell said. The last thing I want to do is turn my good girl bad and see her gone forever.

"I know boo, and I apologize. You deserve better. How can I make it up to you?"

"Well, there is this new Bobbie bag I saw on Rodeo the other day …"

Ahhhh, the makeup bag. See what I mean, how these chicks can be hella expensive. Good thing I got it like that.

"Say no more. Send me the link and I got you, boo."

"OK Daddy."

"Life's too short not to do everyone
you want…"

"BAE, why haven't you called me? You know I miss your big head ass", Bleu said, sounding thirsty as fuck.

"Oh yeah, tell me what else you miss?", I replied in my lowest, most seductive voice.

It was 4 pm on a Wednesday afternoon. Hump Day, as they call it. So, I might as well set something up for later since Curtis is back out of town. Even though my workload has been a killer this week, I'm still gonna make time for that.

Sometimes I think I should slow my roll in between Alex, Bleu, and Curtis. But, life's too short not to do everyone you want. Besides, they should feel lucky to be fucking with me in the first place. I got options. Too many at times.

They don't know the amount of pussy, head, and dick I turn down on a regular basis for them. I'm talking 'bout can't get a decent retail therapy session in without somebody trying to pull out their XYZME card. And don't let me pull up in Black Beauty… all the booty.

"Mmmmmm, I miss the taste of you. Your scent. Your silhouette when I'm hitting it from the back during our late nights… Kinda like tonight."

I love when Bleu uses her words to paint pictures on the canvas that is my mind. Her intellect has always turned me on in ways nobody has been able to touch. But I'd rather she use her mouth in other ways tonight.

"Oh yeah, tonight? What makes you think you got it like that?"

"That lil' moan you tried to hide lets me know I got it like that. So, when are you coming through?"

"Hold on, let me check my schedule", I said knowing damn well I'd clear the whole thing for her.

"How about 11?"

"Bet."

CHAPTER 9
ASS'D OUT

"Because she knows she can't do
what I do and feels the need to
compensate…"

11 PM SEEMS SO FAR AWAY, but I can't be out here looking like a thirsty ass bitch for Bleu. So, I'm gonna do what any normal person would do in this situation - tie up some loose ends at work, go home to freshen up a bit, and bullshit on DistractMe until it's time to head over and get slutted out.

Wanda must be working late tonight and acting like a prude again. I don't know why Bleu puts up with her. Not only does she look 50 when she's in her 30s, but her style game is still stuck in 1999. If Papa Dy-Lan is still doing makeovers, someone please sign this bitch up.

Maybe one day I'll ask Bleu why she's on Wanda so tough. But then again, that's none of my business. I don't give a fuck what goes on in their house, as long as it doesn't come between me and that pretty mouth.

Click clack. Click clack. Went my the bottom of my red heels as I made my way out of Black Beauty, in the elevator, and up to Bleu's place.

Bleu has always been the flashy type, ever since we met in middle school. If she wasn't in Colour Tangent, she stayed dripped in DAPP, Benji Mayne or Fly FaSho. Nowadays the style has upgraded to the highest of fashion, and it looks damn good on her.

Knock knock.

Why the fuck am I knocking for when I have a key? Since Wanda is a traveling nurse and she's hardly ever in town (like Curtis' square ass), Bleu thought it would be a good idea.

But, I rarely use it though… I just don't want to walk in one day and see something I can't unsee. Wanda already can't stand my ass. So, imagine how off the chain she'll be if I bust in one of their sessions.

She's always making her sly remarks regarding me and what I'm doing. But I take it as a compliment because she knows she can't do what I do and feels the need to compensate. Oh well.

Although she knows me as Bleu's bestie, sometimes I get the feeling she knows what's up between us. But how is she ever going to find out, right?

"Hey bae", Bleu grinned, as she let me in smelling like Pussaé, VVS'd down as per usual.

I plopped down on the couch while Bleu poured up two glasses of white wine before we caught up, talking about life, the hustle, and our desire to level up.

Aside from bomb ass head, Bleu is always good for deep convo that inspires me to stunt on these hoes even harder. She's only 2 years older than me, but if we're talking strictly on a soul level, she's got me by a couple of decades.

Five hours and two bottles of wine later, me and Bleu were passed out on the couch with my head on her chest and her arms around me.

We would've probably been knocked out 'til the daylight if it wasn't for this crazy bitch Wanda standing over us with her .22 cocked.

Great, it looks like I'm going to be late to work today.

CHAPTER 10
FEEELINGS

"I don't have time for the hood
politics…"

"BITCH, YOU GOT ME FUCKED UP!", Wanda yelled while aiming straight at my chest.

This bitch must not know who the fuck she's dealing with. From the way she's holding the gun, I can tell she's not 'bout that life. Just in her feelings.

That's one thing I've learned from dealing with women - not only do they notice everything, down to the purple lipstick on the background glass in your dinner plate story, but their emotions cut a million times deeper than a dude's.

Whoever thought of the saying, there's nothing like a

woman scorned must've had hot grits thrown on them. Because this shit is no joke!

"Whoa, whoa. Hol' up baby", Bleu calmly pleaded with Wanda, knowing her emotional ass would do something stupid.

"HOL' UP?! What you want me to hol' up on. Thinking y'all got something going on or blowing this bitch's head off!"

"Come on now, baby. We were just chillin' and had one too many glasses of wine. You know how I get when I'm lit", Bleu said, easing off the couch and slowly walking over to Wanda, hands leading the way.

Good thing I have my smartwatch on today. I usually rock the buss down big face. But something told me to keep it techie tonight and wear my Wonder Watch. Thank God for intuition.

While Bleu was over in the corner trying to talk some sense into a bitch named Wanda, I hit the SOS signal on my watch. Because I will call the police in a New York minute.

I don't have time for the hood politics anymore. The fuck I look like?

CHAPTER 11
OH, NO SHE DIDN'T

"Isn't it crazy how the one's
offering help need it the most…"

"YES SIR, SHE LIVES HERE."

I'm so glad Bleu moved up out of the hood to the good part of town as soon as she got the chance. If she didn't, we'd still be waiting for the police to show up. And Wanda would've been done did something stupid instead of being locked up in the back of a police car, with that hard-ass plastic bench for a backseat… (don't ask).

Whew. What a close call. I haven't had an "incident" in a minute. I thought those days were past me now, but apparently not.

Maybe I should leave Bleu alone. But nah, I can't do

that. Maybe she should leave Wanda alone, for good this time. We all know she's crazy, clearly.

I just want to know who gave her the green light to be in charge of another human being's life when she's a total nutcase herself. Isn't it crazy how the ones offering help need it the most.

"Hey, I'm so sorry that had to happen. I'm through with that bitch. For good this time. Do you want to press charges?", Bleu, looked stressed and solemn, in a daze with her hands over her head.

"Do I want to press charges?! How about I let the bitch get off easy and have someone press her!"

Bleu got me all the way fucked up. Do I want to press charges… that bitch tried to kill me!

"You know what, now is not a good time. I'm just gonna head out and hit you later."

Click clack. Click clack. These hoes get on my nerves.

CHAPTER 12
BOSS LADY

"Funny how karma comes around
to tap that ass when you're bent
over smelling the roses…"

MONDAY, April 7th — 10 AM PST

It's been 3 months since I last saw Bleu, and I really don't care. That still doesn't stop her ol' thirsty ass from spamming my phone though.

You would think that she'd get the message by now. I know it wasn't all her fault and maybe I should stop trippin'. But I'm still mad at the situation she put me in.

She knew that crazy bitch bought a strap during the

summer protests and never told me. Not like having that info that would change anything. But still.

I'm just glad Wanda's crazy ass is still in jail. I kept it G and decided not to press charges. But tell me why this crazy bitch had a warrant out for her arrest. Apparently, she got caught slippin' doing PPP fraud. With her ol' scamming ass.

So, she's been sitting in a cell waiting to go to trial. It's funny how karma comes around to tap that ass when you're bent over smelling the roses.

Knock knock.

"Yes, come in", I answered as Marco, my right-hand man strolled into my office. I was sitting behind my desk looking a lil' dazed, which he immediately picked up on.

"Daydreaming again, boss lady?"

"Ummmmm, no. I was just thinking about how we're going to scale this marketing campaign for our new line. Please tell me that's why you came."

"Actually, I do have some ideas on how we can touch another mill. But that's not why I came. Bleu's in the lobby waiting for you. I told her bounce, but you know she's not trying to hear that."

"Alright, send her this way in 15 minutes. Tell her I'm in a meeting."

I figure that'll buy me enough time to get my thoughts together on where, when, why, and how she got me fucked up. I don't know why she decided to bring her ass up here today, out of all days in the week.

It's Monday for God's sake. Who gets shit done on Monday. Doesn't she have some houses to flip or video games to play?

Anyway, let me see what this bitch wants.

CHAPTER 13
HEAD GAMES

"But when you block a bitch, they
show up at your job…"

"YES BLEU, how may I help you?", was my reply to her
lame-ass comeback line, *"Hey boo, I missed you."*

You'd think after not seeing me for months, she
would have something better to say than hey. I'll just
blame it on her nerves though.

Ever since Bleu's mom suddenly passed, she gets
bad panic attacks that take away her vibrancy. They
were close as fuck. So, she has a lot of irrational fears
about people leaving her life before she's ready to let go.

*"So, you're not going to admit you missed me too? I know
you did and got all my texts. You forgot to turn off your read
receipts."*

Damn. She got me.

"Yeah, I saw your messages. That doesn't mean I have to respond. You put me in a bad spot. Now Wanda's fam is on my ass for shit I had nothing to do with and I gotta interrupt my schedule to hear your lame apology. You should just go on ahead and take that L. Losing me."

"Come on, stop playing games with me," Bleu said, as serious as I'd ever seen her.

"You know I got love for you. You held me down for more than half my life. You helped me study for those finals, get my credit straight and buy my first property. You keep me in the right mental space, feeding my soul when it's sick… I'd lose it if I lost you."

Damn. She got me, again.

"Let me make it up to you. Just tell me how."

Bleu sure does know how to get me weak. After the millionth time of this back and forth, you'd figure I'd just block her to keep the distance. But, when you block a bitch, they want to show up at your job. And if they can't find you there, they start callin' your mama's phone…

I must've been in my head again, because the next thing I know Bleu was in my face, smelling all good 'n shit, leaning in for a kiss.

Should I, or should I? I think yes.

"Lock the door", I moaned before proceeding to get some of the best head of my life.

This bitch is lucky I can't stay mad for long. I hope Marco doesn't hear too much.

CHAPTER 14
PRETTY SAVAGE

"Just because I need someone to
check me once in a while…"

THINGS HAVE BEEN on the up and up between me and Bleu these past few weeks. Curtis is still in his bag and out of town most days. I'm not tripping though because that gives me and Bleu even more time to get it in.

I mean, we spend quality time together too. Especially since Wanda isn't in the picture cock blocking. But there's nothing like getting it in with Bleu's fine ass. Her stroke game is crazy. Head game on fire. And did I mention she's a squirter?

Oooooh. My pussy just jumped a lil' from the thought. I can't wait to get slutted out tonight.

Ring. Ring.

"Hey bae, I've been missing you. Why have you been so MIA on me?"

Damn. I hate to hurt Alex, but what me and Bleu have going on right now runs way deeper. Even though me and Alex have had our lil' what do we call this going on for a year or so, I just don't think she's what I'm looking for.

She's nice, sweet, and a freak. But her mental isn't where I need it to be to hang with me. She's got a whole lot more growing to do and life to live before I would think about kicking things up a notch. She needs to get on her pretty savage shit too. Like ASAP, because I don't see this lasting too much longer.

I've always had a thing for aggressive femmes anyway. Just because I need somebody to check me once in a while. And I just don't think Alex is capable of that. At least not right now.

"Hey boo. I've been real busy with work lately. You know how I just dropped our new collection? We sold out the first day. So, I've been sourcing backup suppliers. It's been crazyyy."

"That's great news! Why don't you stop by my place after work, so I can celebrate you."

Oh shit. What is this new tone? I must admit it's turning me on.

"Mmmmm. That sounds real good right about now. I need to unwind. I'll be done by 7. So, I'll be at your place by 8."

"OK daddy. Don't forget to bring your backpack."

CHAPTER 15
IN MY BAG

> "I really just wanted to go home,
> take a shower, and be on my
> way to knock down Alex's
> walls…"

DAMN. Alex got me in my bag, literally. I don't know when, if ever this girl has made me this damn horny.

It was 4 pm when I got off the phone, and I was done with work by 5:30. I knocked it out so fast, Marco asked if I was off that shit.

But I really just wanted to go home, take a shower, and be on my way to knock Alex's walls down. Fuck a 8 pm.

Good thing my office isn't too far away from where I stay. I'm surprised I didn't get a speeding ticket on my way here, with the way I was whippin' Black Beauty down the 101.

"Damn, it feels good when you stroke on it. Wouldn't you love if I come all up in you". Man, this playlist never gets old. Alex really doesn't know what she got herself into, talking to me like that.

"Slide downtown. Knock on the door. The right place is my face..." Yassss, come through freak nasty New Jack Swing! Did I say this playlist never gets old?

It was a good 40 minutes before I got home. That rush hour traffic is no joke. I still love my city though. Moving away has never been a thought. Even though those houses in Atlanta sure do look good, I could never see myself living anywhere else but in the sunshine.

"Hey Cutie! I missed you so much!!"

Unlike these dumb dudes and indecisive women, Cutie my Red Poodle always makes me happy. I love her so much.

"Hey boss lady, how's your day?", asked Q, my housekeeper (thee best housekeeper) before I ran upstairs and hopped in the shower, thinking about what I'm 'bout do to that ass.

Should I hit it from the back or let her ride my face first? Reverse cowgirl or missionary so I can see all of Alex's fuck faces? Edge her or hit the scissors and make her squirt so good she needs new sheet sets? How about all of the above for $500, Bob? I got the time today.

Fuck. I must've got too caught up in my thoughts

because the next thing I know it's 8 o'clock and I'm running late.

Good thing I left work early. Even better that Alex lives in the valley too. So, it won't be long before I'm deep diving in that ocean. *"See you later, Q!"*, I called out before grabbing a bite to eat and my strap on my way out the door.

CHAPTER 16
#143

"Anticipation is a mutha…"

RING. Ring. Ring.

Got damn. Why does this intercom always take so long to connect? I don't have time for this shit. Not today! I'm trying to be waist-deep in some pussy right now. Not waiting outside like I'm delivering for FeedMeNow.

No click clack, click clack tonight. I'm on my real nigga shit. I got my mids on, hair tied in a bun, backpack packed, and a fifth of that Yak. Because, like the great street philosopher, Tell Me More said, "*If you stay on swivel, you don't gotta get in they ass*". Amen.

Buzz.

Finally! I've been waiting out here for 5 minutes and

am even hornier than I was on the drive over here. Good thing I decided to leave my P.S. panties at home. I'm sure they would've been soaking wet by now. Anticipation is a mutha.

Now, let me try to remember which floor Alex is on. It's been so long, and I'm always getting them confused. I don't want to call her and look like these lame dudes out here that just want the pussy and don't care enough to remember your apartment number. But then again, she knows what the fuck is going on.

OK. OK. I think this is it: #143.

Knock. Knock.

I hope she remembers to do that little thing I like.

CHAPTER 17
HARDWOOD FLOORS

"Keep your legs up or I'm gonna
have to stop…"

"COME IN, IT'S OPEN."

"Hey boo, where ya at?", I called out as I made my way into Alex's apartment and was immediately captured by her signature, soft and flowery fragrance. Alex's place always smells so nice, so feminine. I love it.

"Right here. In the bedroom, bae."

"OK. I'm coming."

But I really should've said "I'm running" with the way I slipped and almost broke my neck while dashing down Alex's hardwood floor hallway. On second thought, maybe I shouldn't have taken my shoes off at the door.

But it's OK because Alex's room has carpet, plus the canopied California King size bed I got her for V Day. If I can't make it do what it do with that setup, then I need my ass beat.

It wasn't before long until I reached my destination and was standing in front of the doorway of the candle-lit room. Pretty In The Kitty's "She Like The Way I Rearrange Them Guts" playing softly in the background.

OK, I'm feeling this!

Alex is a real girly girl, with her hair 24/7 laid, a full set, and fresh face beat. The whole nine. Real submissive too. But not tonight. So, I know it's about to go down. I don't know what or who got into her since I've been gone, but I like it.

"Hey Daddy, I missed you", Alex whispered in my ear while pulling me into her warmth, perfectly manicured hands climbing inside my grey fuckboy sweats that now had a dark spot in the middle.

"Mmmmmm. Daddy's good girl missed me?"

"Ummmm hmm. Let me show you how much", Alex said before grabbing my bag and digging around to find what she asked for, not knowing how bad she's about to get it.

But right when I was about to get up and give her the business, Alex pushed me back down and strapped up, giving me the most freak-nastiest, mischievous look I've ever seen.

"Keep your legs up or I'm gonna have to stop", Alex whispered in my ear.

And she has on that little thing I like. Damn, it's about to be a wild night.

CHAPTER 18
PIECES ON THE BOARD

"If a playa had a wish right now…"

"GOOD MORNING BAE. How was your sleep?"

I still can't believe it's Friday already, again. How did I let the week slip away from me? I got shit done, of course. But this week in particular has been a blur.

Ever since Alex slutted me out last Thursday, I've been in my head more than ever. Like damn. Where did she learn those moves? Who has she been fucking? And how am I going to split whatever little free time I have between Bleu, Curtis, and now Alex? If a playa had a wish right now it would be to make two or three more of me because the thought is exhausting.

"Hey boo, my sleep was great. Looking forward to seeing you tomorrow."

Coordinating my summer collection's release party has been a challenge. Aside from the city being close to going back on lockdown and me having to switch venues at the last minute, the caterer pulled out due to catching Rona, along with a lot of the performers.

I wasn't about to throw the damn thing, to tell the truth. But I already paid for the marketing campaign and have some celebs coming through. So, fuck it.

To top it off, I've been so distracted with all the drama that I accidentally told all my boos about the party. Well, they would've known when they got on DistractMe anyway because I dumped a couple racks into ads too. Gotta do it big, ya know.

How am I going to move with Bleu, Curtis, and Alex all in the room though? Maybe I'll just keep mingling all night, so they don't have a chance to see me with the others and start asking questions. Or how about I have my videographer follow me around all night, so they won't want to come near and interrupt…

"Bae, are you still there?"

"Ummm, yeah. I was just thinking about how excited I am to see you in the dress I bought you. But Marco needs my help with something. I'll talk to you later."

"OK. Byeeeeeee."

CHAPTER 19
STAR STRUCK

"She just knows me as Paid Bae..."

NEVER IN A MILLION years did I think my life would be like this. I'm doing everything (and everyone) I love, hit the 8-figure mark, and have the type of respect nobody can buy. Plus, my weekends are always poppin'.

Even though I'm about to walk into this club with a slight sense of dread, nobody will ever know because you can never let 'em see you sweat. Especially me.

I'm glad I decided to get here early, so I can have a bird's eye view of everybody making their entrance. I got love for all my boos. But not today and definitely not at a time like this.

If some shit between us is going to pop off, I'll be

damned if it happens on one of the biggest nights of my life. I'm not trying to end up on ConfusionCorner tomorrow.

Bleu said she'll be here at 9, which we all know means 10:30. And Alex is on the way, which means right on time. Man, I'm really starting to fall for her square ass. Who knows when Curtis will show up. If he even decides to come. He's been acting hella funny this month. He might think he's slick, but I pick up on everything. Energy included.

Damn. Damn. Damn. Here comes Alex, looking good as ever. Did her ass get thicker? Or has it just been the way I've been beating them cheeks. I'd like to think the latter because Alex takes all the D like a pro, you'd never know. And the upside is no babies.

Sometimes I wonder what type of mom I would be. All I know is my kids would be fly as fuck. Maybe Alex can be my baby mama because I damn sure am not about to carry no...

"Hey bae!", screamed Alex, waving extra hard and running over like a starstruck groupie. You can't blame her though, she's never been in this type of environment.

She might know how I groove, but she's never had a chance to see me move. She just knows me as "Paid Bae" that can get and give her whatever she wants. Shit, I wouldn't ask any questions either.

"Heyyyyyy", I replied while reaching over for a side

hug, hoping the nonchalance of it all would downplay Alex's position in my life to onlookers. I can't have anybody asking me questions.

"*Bae. Everything looks so nice! Thanks for inviting me!! Is that Lil' Billie Beige over there at the bar?! OMG!!*", screamed Alex.

"*Thank you, I appreciate you coming out*", I mumbled, but was really thinking, "Damn girl, on second thought maybe I shouldn't invite you to any more work parties."

I wasn't trying to embarrass ol' girl like that though. So, I just replied, "*Yeah, I think so. Want me to introduce you?*", hoping Billie B would keep her occupied for the night.

"*OMG, yes. Please!*"

Just as I was about to walk over to make the introduction, I spotted Bleu making her way down the red carpet, looking fly as fuck in her suit and Italian gator loafers. Hopefully, she doesn't see Alex all doe-eyed and hugged up on me. I wonder if the bar is open yet … double shots of that dark me, please!

"I might as well fully hop over the
fence and ride the rainbow…"

THANK God I got a step and repeat, and Bleu is one vain muthafucka. She must've spent a good 40 minutes taking pictures and fielding questions from the press before making her way inside.

I managed to ditch Alex with Billie B and get two shots of that dark before running into Bleu.

"Well, look at you. Just doing the damn thing. I'm proud of you", Bleu said with a slight twinkle in her eyes.

She's seen me work and actually witnessed me build my empire from the ground up. But, it wasn't until tonight that she recognized the magnitude of it all.

Maybe it was the caliber of press that came out or the corporate sponsors. Who knows, but she sure was looking at me different tonight. In a good way, of course.

"Yeah, you know me. Just out here making it do what it do", I joked before motioning Marco to come over before he got busy with something else.

"What's up Marco. My girl told me you were a big help in putting tonight together. Major props."

Marco must've been caught off guard by Bleu's compliment because all he could do is smile. I'm sure he thinks Bleu doesn't like him. But looks can be deceiving. She's just very protective when it comes to me and the company I keep.

"Yeah, Marco did such a wonderful job on everything tonight, including booking Lil' Billie Beige. I'm sure he can tell you all about it", I said in my most eager voice, hoping it'd get them both excited so I could make my exit.

"For real, mayne? Billie B is my favorite rapper! How'd you pull that off?!", Bleu said with an excitement I rarely hear. She must've pre-gamed in the car.

Score! Now with Alex and Bleu out of the way, all I have to worry about is Curtis. He must have another bitch on the side, and part of me doesn't even care. I might as well fully hop over the fence and ride the rainbow because he's just not doing it for me anymore.

Aside from being gone all the time, all he does lately

is complain about what I'm doing or not doing. Do I look like the type to stay at home cooking, cleaning, and making him come all day? I should've listened to Bleu. Niggas ain't shit… But hold up, I think that's him at the door.

"Why didn't you tell me? She's
thick as fuck…"

MAYBE I SHOULDN'T HAVE HAD those shots at the bar because my drunk ass thought one of the background dancers was Curtis. Shit like this always happens when I get faded. But how else was I supposed to stay calm with both my boos in the same room?

"Heyyy bae!"

Damn. Damn. Damn. I gotta get this girl outta here, ASAP. What time did me and Marco agree this was over?

"Hey, how was your time with Billie? He's always such a character…", I said, leading the way to the bar, not giving Alex enough time to respond.

"Get whatever you want, it's open bar."

"OK bae. I love you!", Alex gushed.

OMG. What?! See, this is why I don't tell chicks what I do. They start acting funny. I knew Alex loved me a long time ago though. I just find it funny that it's all starting to come out now. We're going to have to talk later. But I'll worry about that tomorrow because here comes Bleu.

"Yoooo, who's that crazy bih saying she loves you?", Bleu laughed, being accustomed to the groupie love I get on nights like these.

"Oh, that's my boo, Alex."

Ooops. Definitely shouldn't have had those shots.

"Girl, what. Why didn't you tell me? She's thick as fuck! Let's set something up for tonight."

From the way she was talking, I could tell Bleu already found her way to the open bar.

We've had a couple of ménages before, but they were all with randoms. The thought of getting served by Alex and Bleu at the same time made my pussy do a little 90s R&B singer dance in the rain.

Oh yes. It's about to go down! Now let me figure out how to get Alex's panties as wet as mine.

"This pussy I'm about to get into
will more than make up for it…"

IT WAS a headache trying to make my way over to the bar. Not only was the venue starting to get packed, but the open bar had everybody on 10. My clubbin' days served me well though, as I slid through the crowd with grace and ease, not knocking over anyone's drink.

"OMG! Was that Bleu Billions you were talking to?! I loveeee her!"

Double score! Looks like the deal is already sealed, I thought while making my way over to the end of the bar where Alex was babysitting her triple shot on the rocks.

"Yeah boo, me and Bleu go way back. Want to meet her?"

"OMG!! Yesss!", Alex screamed so loud a couple of people broke their necks trying to see what was going on, with their ol' nosey-lookin' asses.

"OK. Let's go", I whispered in Alex's ear to make sure she heard me over all the noise.

The warm sensation on her neck and the smell of my fragrance must've turned her on, because when I started leading the way to where Bleu was standing by the stage, Alex was on my ass. All I could feel was her soft hands sliding up in between my legs, near the edge of my wetness.

Good thing it's dark in here, and the open bar has everybody lit. I'm not trying to be on OMGDidYouSeeThat tomorrow, talking 'bout I was spotted with a new love interest in compromising positions.

But fuck it, I don't care anymore. If I end up on ConfusionCorner in the morning, then so be it. This pussy I'm about to get into will more than make up for it.

"Hey Bleu, I'd like to introduce you to Alex. She's a huge fan of what you do", I said trying to sound as chill as possible.

"Nice to meet you, Alex. I recognize you from earlier in the night. Is that the new dress from BayYang's summer collection?"

Wait, hold up. I know Bleu isn't trying to game my girl!

"Excuse me, boss lady. I need to speak with you for a minute", Marco suddenly interrupted.

When did he get here? I was so caught up in the poly possibilities, I didn't even notice him walking over. It must be something serious though because he knows not to interrupt my mackin'.

"Excuse me ladies, I'll be right back."

"I already know when that
"Coochie Beast" beat drops it'll
be epic…"

"*DAMN MARCO, I was working on setting something up for tonight. What's the deal?*", I said, sounding more annoyed than anything.

"*My bad. The Sheriff was outside trying to shut us down, talking about we're over capacity, which I know is cap*", Marco replied with a slightly deflated look on his face.

What the fuck! I knew we should've thrown the party on La Brea, instead of out here with all these bougie, no fun having mofos.

"*Where are they at? Let me talk to them*", I cut Marco off, while heading for the door. I don't know who called the police on me, but they can catch these hands. I worked too hard on tonight for it to be shut down before Hood Doll performs. I already know when that "Coochie Beast" beat drops it'll be epic.

"Don't trip boss lady, I already took care of it. Just thought I'd let you know", Marco calmly reassured me.

Marco is weird like that. Why would he pull me out mid-conversation just to tell me some shit like that? I could've been on my way to some good pussy and mouth by now. Sometimes I think he just needs validation and some more deposits in the confidence department. Things I can't give right now.

"OK, thanks Marco. Tell them bring over two more bottles. I'll be next to the stage, near Bleu. And oh yeah, I'm about to head out. So, hold it down for me", I called out.

"Gotcha, boss lady."

"Why wait for him when I have two
perfectly available pussies to
play with…"

I DON'T KNOW whether to be pissed or elated that Alex and Bleu hit it off so well. On one hand, that means less convincing on my part. But on the other, what if they get too caught up in each other tonight and leave me laying there having to handle my own business while watching them bust the nuts I deserve? I set up this play. I need to be the one bustin' the nuts here!

But, let me not get too far ahead of myself. Maybe the chemistry is just that good. Maybe we can make this a love triad. Fuck Curtis, with his always out-of-town ass. Why wait for him when I have two perfectly available pussies to play with whenever I want. Curtis sure does have me fucked up. I hope he is seeing someone else. That way I'll have a perfectly good reason to leave.

"My bad. I had to put out a little fire. I see you two managed to start one of your own while I was away", I interrupted Bleu and Alex's little kekeing session, trying to take the saltiness out of my tone.

"Oh yeah, Alex was just telling me about the new ride you copped her, the Hybrid F Sympa. I'm impressed", Bleu said. But I wasn't buying it. I know her game all too well. She was probably talking about how she wanted to see how big the back seats are.

"Yeah, you know how I do. Go big or go home. Did you hit the valet tonight, Alex?", I replied.

"Yes Daddy, just like how you said. I don't want you drinking and driving tonight. You already look like you've had enough", Alex chimed in.

And with perfect timing, our two black bottles arrived.

"I'm cool. But I'm glad you drove today. With the way those curves are hitting, I'm not sure I'd be able to keep my eyes on the road", I slyly replied.

"Yes, I agree. That body is looking awfully right tonight, girl", Bleu softly sang, letting me know to take both bottles with us out the door.

Alex blushed more from Bleu's comment than mine,

which made me feel some type of way. But it's ok, is what I'm going to keep telling myself.

"Awwww, thanks Bleu. And Zaddy too. I just wish I could have the both of you right now", Alex blurted, before she could catch herself.

I know it was all her and not the liquor talking because that glass she was babysitting all night was still filled up to the top. Actually, a little more overflowing than before, since the ice started to melt.

It was at that point when me and Bleu's locked eyes, and we knew it was on.

"Marco, call me an Extra Grande!"

CHAPTER 25
MIND YOURS

"I thought for a split second he
could be my Zaddy…"

GETTING Marco to order me an Extra Grande Noir for the trip back to my place was the best decision I made all night. Even though Alex drove and had her car waiting in valet, I wanted to spice up the night with her, me, and Bleu in the backseat.

It must've been one hot Saturday night because I swore it took at least an hour for them to pull up. I wasn't trippin' though because that gave me time to introduce our new line and bring out Hood Doll to perform "Coochie Beast". It was epic, just like I thought. Our live went crazy!

It's also crazy how everything works out for the

good in the end, always. I really need to stop overthinking things, and get out of my head and into reality more often. It's not that serious. And besides, nothing ever plays out the way I imagine.

Hopefully, that doesn't ring true tonight though, because what I'm imagining is about to be like that Ryané song, "Private Pounding".

"Aye bae, you good?", Bleu tapped me on my shoulder while we were waiting outside for the Grande to pull up.

"Oh, yeah. I'm cool. Just thinking about how it's about to go down. From the front… to the back… on the counter… over the balcony…", I said, being abruptly pulled from my daydreaming session.

"Mmmmmm. That all sounds good daddy", Alex said, one arm wrapped around mine, while the other ran down between my legs.

"Yeahhhh, that sounds very good", Bleu came up from behind, whispering in my ear while some nosey ass kids with camera phones captured the whole scene.

Damn. Damn. Damn! Can I catch a break?

Oh well, fuck it. Good thing I have an amazing publicist on my team. She'll fix everything by the morning. It took a cool minute to build, but I love my team. If she can pull this off, I don't mind her taking her two-week trip to Tanzania.

"For Susan?", I asked as the Extra Grande pulled up. I never give out my government name on apps like this.

Because people are crazy and the last thing I need is some psycho looking me up and knowing where I live. Fuck that.

"Yes ma'am", an older Black gentleman replied, with his hat cocked slightly to the side and a demeanor so smooth, I thought for a second he could be my Zaddy.

"OK, great. Here's a little something to keep your eyes on the road", I said slipping him a C note, while we all slid in the second row.

With me in the middle, Bleu's fingers pushed deep inside my pussy and my breasts in Alex's mouth, the ride home got interesting as soon as we pulled off into the obscurity of another warm LA night.

CHAPTER 26

WHIPPIN' 101

"It's about to get loud and messy.
Just the way I like it…"

FLYING DOWN the 101 freeway after midnight is always a ride. It would've been even better if I was riding some pussy in the backseat. But that would all have to wait until we pull up to my place, which was only another 12 minutes away.

I knew the exact time because I kept locking eyes with Mr. Extra Grande Driver before he would abruptly look down at his GPS. He knows damn well he would love to get in on this action. But, I digress.

I almost came about twice too. Good thing Bleu knows how to edge me right. Alex on the other hand…

Ring. Ring. Ring.

Oh, hell no. I know it's not that nigga Curtis calling me. Not only did I fail to see his face on the biggest night of my career, he has the audacity to be calling me during booty call hours. Oh hell no.

*Decline

"Yo, put your phone on silent. Fuck that nigga", Bleu whispered in my ear.

But part of me can't resist at least seeing what Curtis wants before I bust all these nuts in Bleu's pretty pink mouth.

"Hey bae, sorry I couldn't make it out tonight. Got caught up with work. I'll make it up to you, for sure. Just let me know when you get home", read Curtis' text.

I know this LAME ass nigga did not just use my line, on me! The audacity. He better be glad I have some pussy to tend to. That's the only thing keeping me from tossing all his shit in a trash can and "feening to inhale" it.

"Bae, is something wrong?", Alex looked up at me with a hint of concern. My body must've tensed up from the thought of Curtis' antics.

"No, I'm good. Just keep going", I fake moaned to divert her attention.

I can't believe this is happening. First, Curtis throws his negative energy on my party by being a no-call, no-show. Now he's getting in the way of me and my pussy. That's it. This is where I draw the line.

If I was high, it would've been blown the minute I

saw his ugly ass picture on my phone screen. It's ok though is what I'm still going to tell myself.

Thank God my place is right around the corner. Hopefully, Q is knocked out in her quarters because it's about to get loud and messy. Just the way I like it.

CHAPTER 27

SIMPIN' WHEN WET

"Damn! Will y'all bring both y'all
fine ass inside so you can come
get the business…"

"*HERE WE ARE, ladies. Enjoy the rest of your night, and thank you for the show*", Mr. Extra Grande Driver said, while tipping his hat off to me.

No, this nigga did not just say thank you for the show. What the fuck kind of night is this. Why did I pay him $100 for him to get his penile-enhancement-infused dick up.

Well, I hope he busts several nuts tonight at the thought of what he just got to experience. It must've been the most action he's had in decades. He is pretty fine though. So, maybe not. I should get his number…

"Come on, bae! I want you deep inside of me", Alex whimpered, pulling me from the depth of my thoughts and clean out the back of the black SUV.

Bleu must've got the memo light years ago because my front door was already hanging wide open. I hope she sets up everything just how I like.

I also still must be pretty faded by the way I fell out the Grande from Alex's tug. She wanted me bad, and it showed.

The feeling was mutual. I was so wet from our backseat shenanigans, I almost broke a hip walking to the front door.

Good thing Alex was there for me to lean on. She's actually always there for me to lean on. Maybe I should wife her. Shit, I already bought the girl a Hybrid F Sympa. A fuckin' F Sympa. Like who does that...

"Damn! Will y'all bring both y'all fine ass inside so you can come get the business", Bleu called out with a black bottle in her right hand.

I knew her ass was in there doing something. In a minute she'll be doing me, just the way I like. But first, let us get inside the house before my nosey-ass neighbors wake up.

CHAPTER 28
2-FOR-1 SPECIAL

"Alex is gonna have to learn how to
hang if she wants to fuck with
what me and Bleu got
going on…"

"YO' pussy been on my mind. I bet it sound wetter on my face…", D1 Trilla sure does know how to set the tone right, with his freaky-ass music. Him, Buff, Calmer Keys, and Simi Simeon all be on that freak shit. I love it! It must be a million babies made off their tracks every year.

"Because it is", Bleu came up from behind, rubbing on my clit, as the record played, and we waited for Alex to finish freshening up in the bathroom.

"Damn Alex, if you don't hurry yo ass up outta that

bathroom", I thought while me and Bleu got it started. I usually have manners when it comes to things like this, but Alex is gonna have to learn how to hang if she wants to fuck with what me and Bleu got going on.

I don't know how much time passed before Alex came out the bathroom. What the fuck was she doing in there for so long. Coke?

I know she dabbled a bit when she was in college, so I wouldn't put it past her. She got me fucked up if she thinks I'm about to support a coke habit though. That last bitch damn near ran me dry.

"Sorry bae. It was a little wetter down there than I thought", Alex said while walking over to the bed in her birthday suit.

Damn, her body doesn't have to be bangin' like that!

"Girl, you know I'll clean you up nice and right. You didn't have to do all that", I seductively said while motioning her over to the bed, where me and Bleu were laying.

Alex smiled, with that look in her eyes. You know the one where you know it's about to go all the way down.

Bleu was strapped up. And I was playing with my pussy, getting ready for the 2-for-1. Alex already knew what was on my mind with the way she put that pussy on my face and my tongue slid deep inside, right before Bleu got ready to slide deep inside me.

"I hope y'all are ready for Daddy's dick", Bleu said with that pretty mouth of hers.

"Yes Daddy", Me and Alex said in unison.

"And I hope you're ready to go to heaven", Curtis said while standing in the doorway with his Glock 19.

Oh God, not this shit again.

CHAPTER 29
SLIDE LEFT

"Mayne, fuck you and all y'all dyke
ass bitches…"

"I'M NOT ready to go nowhere, nigga!", Bleu growled, reaching for her gun on the nightstand.

See, we both knew Curtis wasn't about to do shit. The gun didn't even have bullets. He just liked to use it to scare people. With his lame ass.

I've been having thoughts of leaving Curtis for months now. This just confirms everything. He's just become too embarrassing and emotionally unavailable to deal with. Why would I say with someone like that? His fly no longer matches mine, plus he's just plain disrespectful these days. It's sad. But, growing apart is a part of life.

"*It ain't my fault you can't satisfy your woman. She's mine now, nigga!*", Bleu belted out.

Ooooooh, my pussy did a lil' jump. I love it when Bleu takes control and lets a nigga know what's up! Yasssss, she's getting all this pussy tonight.

"*Mayne, fuck you and all y'all dyke ass bitches. You can keep that. The pussy was trash anyway!*", Curtis whimpered.

"*Fuck you nigga! This is the best pussy you've ever had and will ever get!! Now get the fuck out my house with your ol' square havin' ass!*", I yelled across the room, hurling a pillow at his head.

"*Fuck you bitch!*", Curtis said while lunging towards me before Bleu cocked her .22 and he ran down the stairs.

It was at that point me and Bleu chuckled, noticing Alex in the corner naked, looking scared, amused, and turned on at the same time.

"*Who was that bae?*", she finally blurted out while walking over to the California King.

"*Don't worry about it, boo. Just someone from my past that can't get passed what I'm serving*", I said with a laugh hoping to throw Alex off and keep her water flowing.

"*Yeah, don't worry 'bout him. Worry about these back shots you're about to get*", Bleu chimed in while bending Alex over the front of the bed, as I spread my legs open for her to get a taste.

"Hold on" I moaned out to them both.
"Lemme get my camera…"

TO BE CONTINUED

A WORD FROM THE AUTHOR

Whew. What a story! My intent with SIMC is to shine a light on lesser-known stories. Not only in the Black community, but in Los Angeles and the LGBTQ+ world as well. I hope you got a kick out of the messy, real, and rawness.

Get excited because return of the real is here! Let's run it up and continue letting our lights shine bright. Because boss chicks make the world go 'round, and this is only the beginning.

- Keish Monique

ABOUT KEISH MONIQUE

Keish Monique is a Los Angeles-bred, multi-hyphenate creative and serial entrepreneur. Growing up in various parts of the city, including View Park aka Black Beverly Hills and South Central LA, as well as attending the equally popular Westchester and Crenshaw high schools, Keish brings a unique perspective to the Urban Fiction space.

When she's not with her pen or lost in thought, Keish can be found enjoying the finer things in life, such as indulging in personal development, playing outside, and serving as CEO/Editor-In-Chief of Hype Off Life magazine.

KEEP IN TOUCH

Website: keishmonique.com

Email: hey@keishmonique.com

Instagram: @lowkeyinlosangeles

TikTok: @lowkeyinlosangeles

Facebook: WestCoast Keish

IT'S THE REVIEWS FOR ME

If you enjoyed "Squares In My Circle", please leave me a review and tell two friends to tell a friend. I'd love to hear your thoughts!

https://www.amazon.com/review/create-review?asin=B0BSGLNK66

BONUS

Gain Exclusive Access to The "BangHers" Playlist
Curated by Keish Monique